Retold by
Nancy Van Laan

Illustrated by
Beatriz Vidal

RAINBOW CROW

A Lenape Tale

Dragonfly Books · Alfred A. Knopf
New York

For my parents, who encouraged me to wonder,
and for the Lenape people,
who taught me the wonder of all living things
— N. V. L.

Para Pablo, Mariana, y Federico
— B. V.

A DRAGONFLY BOOK PUBLISHED BY ALFRED A. KNOPF, INC.

Text copyright © 1989 by Nancy Van Laan. Illustrations copyright © 1989 by Beatriz Vidal.

All rights reserved under International and Pan-American Copyright Conventions. Published in the United States
by Alfred A. Knopf, Inc., New York, and simultaneously in Canada by Random House of Canada Limited, Toronto.
Distributed by Random House, Inc., New York. Originally published in hardcover by Alfred A. Knopf, Inc.,
in 1989. Book design by Mina Greenstein.

Manufactured in Singapore   10 9 8 7 6 5 4 3 2 1

Library of Congress Cataloging-in-Publication Data
Van Laan, Nancy. Rainbow crow / by Nancy Van Laan ; illustrated by Beatriz Vidal.
p.   cm. Summary: When the weather changes and the ever-falling snow threatens to engulf all the animals,
it is Crow who flies up to receive the gift of fire from the Great Sky Spirit.   ISBN 0-394-89577-0
ISBN 0-394-99577-5 (lib. bdg.) ISBN 679-81942-8 (pbk.)   1. Indians of North America—Legends. 2. Fire—
Folklore—Juvenile literature.
[1. Indians of North America—Legends.   2. Fire—Folklore.]   I. Vidal, Beatriz, ill.   II. Title.   E98.F6V36   1989
398.2'6—dc19   [E]   88-12967

AUTHOR'S NOTE

Several years ago, at a corn-planting ceremony near my home in Bucks County, Pennsylvania, I was captivated listening to a Lenape Elder, Bill "Whippoorwill" Thompson. Beneath the trees, to a gathering of young and old, he told the stories of his people—including the legend of Rainbow Crow.

Crow, also known as Raven, had always intrigued me. First, its size: large and powerful; second, its temperament: haughty, sly, and mischievous; third, its intelligence: fierce and daring; and finally, its wonderful sense of humor. When I heard this legend, I was surprised to discover yet another characteristic: its bravery. And I was eager to write the tale down.

Several legends from different tribes depict Crow as Fire Bearer. But as far as I know, the Lenape is the only one that describes Crow as a bird with rainbow-colored feathers. An exotic, brilliantly plumed bird, the paroquet, at one time did thrive in eastern Pennsylvania, the Lenape's homeland. Interestingly, maize was a favorite food of both birds. Perhaps the presence of the multicolored paroquet in the land of the Lenape inspired the original teller to choose a rainbow-colored crow.

Today, Bill Thompson is Rainbow Crow's official teller. It has been handed down in his family, from father to son, for countless generations. I am indebted to Bill for giving me permission to adapt it for publication; and I hope that, through my retelling, a wide, new audience will come to know this beautiful Lenape legend.

Long, long ago, before the Two-Legged
walked the Earth, the weather was always warm and the
animals were always happy.

But one day something happened to cause the Earth to grow cold. Tiny crystals, glittering like diamonds, drifted down from the sky, covering Earth with a sparkling softness.

The animals, seeing snow for the first time, were not afraid.

But soon the snow deepened and Mouse disappeared.
The tip of his tail was all the animals could see, and they
began to worry.

Then Rabbit disappeared. The tips of his ears were all the animals could see, and they worried more.

At last they gathered together in a clearing deep inside the forest to talk about the weather. What was needed, they decided, was a messenger to travel at once to the Great Sky Spirit and ask him to stop the snow. But who would be willing to leave Earth to visit the distant place where the Sky Spirit dwelled?

Possum said, "Owl is the wisest. Perhaps he should go."

"But no," the animals whispered. "He might get lost in the light of day. So Owl should not go."

Then Beaver said, "Perhaps Raccoon should go."

"But no," the animals argued. "He might follow his tail instead of his nose. So Raccoon should not go."

Then Skunk said, "Perhaps Coyote should go."

"But no!" the animals shouted. "Coyote is clever and loves to play tricks. He might chase the clouds or swallow the wind. So Coyote should not go."

"Scritcha, scritcha, screetcha, scratcha,
Yippa, yappa, yow hi yowl!"

The noisy animals screeched and howled because they could not decide who should visit the Great Sky Spirit to ask him to stop the snow.

And so the snow grew deeper and deeper and deeper, and the small animals climbed on top of the tall animals so they would not disappear.

Suddenly, down from the top of the tallest tree, flew Rainbow Crow, the most beautiful bird on Earth, who called out to all of the animals below in the sweetest voice of all birds. And he sang:

"I will go. I will stop the snow."

And the animals, happy at last to have Crow as their messenger, chanted a song of praise:

"Aiya, aiya, aiya, aiya,
Rain, Rainbow Crow,
Stop the snow, Crow.
Fly to the sky high,
Rain, Rainbow Crow,
Aiya, aiya, aiya, aiya."

Then high up into the sky flew Rainbow Crow, far above the snow and the winds of the Earth, way beyond the moon, the stars, and the clouds.

For three days Crow flew, until he came upon the Great Sky Spirit, who was too busy to notice. So Rainbow Crow began to sing:

> "O Great Spirit in the Sky,
> You rule the Earth from way up high.
> You make the creatures, large and small,
> You are the ruler of us all.
> You make the trees and flowers grow,
> You cause the wind and clouds to blow,
> You make the rain, you make the snow,
> You make the cold on Earth below.
> O Great Spirit in the Sky,
> For you, I sing this lullaby."

The Great Spirit stopped to listen. Never before had he heard such a sweet voice sing such a beautiful song. And he told Crow to choose a gift. Now, Crow knew that far below on Earth the snow was getting so deep that soon all the animals would disappear. So he asked the Great Spirit to stop the snow.

The Great Spirit replied, "No, Crow, I cannot stop the snow, for snow has a spirit of its own. When Snow Spirit leaves the clouds to visit with his friend Wind Spirit, the snow will stop, but Earth will still be cold."

So Crow asked the Great Spirit to stop the cold. The Great Spirit replied, "No, Crow, I cannot stop the cold. All I can do is give you the gift of Fire. Fire will keep you warm and will melt the snow so that your friends will be content until warm weather returns."

The Great Spirit picked up a stick, put a bit of Fire on the end of it, and handed it to Crow. "I will give you this gift but once. Hurry, fly back to Earth before the Fire disappears."

Off flew Crow.

On the first day, as Crow flew down, showering sparks of Fire darkened his tail feathers.

On the second day, as Crow flew down, the Fire burned brighter and the stick grew shorter, and all of Crow's feathers were covered with soot.

On the third day, as Crow flew down, the Fire was so hot and the stick was so short that smoke and ash blew into Crow's mouth, and his voice became cracked and hoarse.

"Caw, caw...."

And when at last Crow returned to the clearing in the forest, all the animals had disappeared. Only the tops of the tallest trees could be seen, their branches sprouting through the deep snow. So Crow flew down, close to the pale, pale ground, around and around until the Fire melted the snow and his friends were safe.

And this tiny stick of Fire became the grandfather of all fires, and for this all the animals on Earth thanked Crow. They danced and chanted a song of praise:

"Aiya, aiya, aiya, aiya,
Kind, young, brave Crow
Saved us from snow,
Flew to the sky high,
Brought back Fire,
Now just plain Crow,
No more rainbow,
Aiya, aiya, aiya, aiya."

At last Crow, all alone, flew off to a distant tree, where he wept. He was no longer beautiful. He could no longer sing a sweet song. His rainbow feathers were gone forever.

When Snow Spirit emptied the clouds and joined Wind Spirit, the snow stopped. But Crow still wept.

The Great Sky Spirit heard Crow and came down from the sky. And when he saw Crow, he said, "Soon the Two-Legged will appear on Earth. He will take the Fire and be master of all but you. For being so brave and unselfish, I give you the gift of Freedom:

"*The Two-Legged will never hunt you,*
For your meat tastes like fire and smoke.

The Two-Legged will never capture you,
For your beautiful voice is now crackly and hoarse.

The Two-Legged will never want your feathers,
Because your rainbow colors are now black.

But your black feathers will shine
And they will reflect all the colors on Earth.
If you look closely, you will see."

Then Crow looked, and he saw hundreds of tiny rainbows shining in his black feathers, and he was content.

The Great Spirit returned to his home in the distant sky, and Crow happily returned to his friends in the forest, proud that he was now Black Crow, with shining feathers full of tiny rainbows.